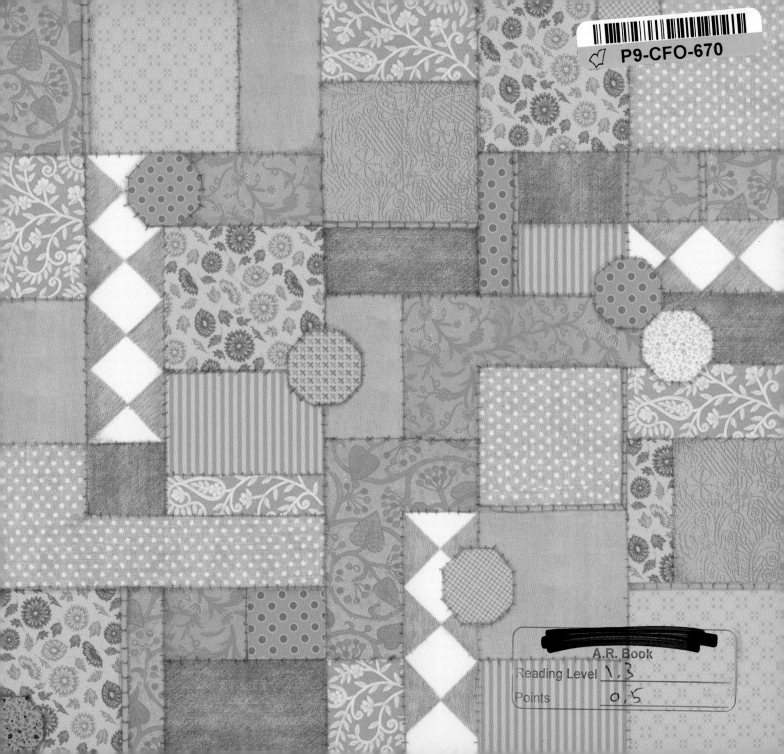

A.R. Book
Reading Level 1.3
Points 0.5

Hedgehog's Magic Tricks

Ruth Paul

C P
CANDLEWICK PRESS

Hedgehog does magic tricks.
His first helper is Mouse.

Hedgehog is going to make
Mouse disappear.

"Abracadabra!"
says Hedgehog.

"Am I still here?" asks Mouse.

Hedgehog tries again.
This time his helper is Rabbit.

But where is Rabbit?

"Abracadabra!" says Hedgehog.
And he makes Rabbit appear.

"Ouch!"
says Rabbit.

Now Hedgehog needs a new helper, to get inside the box.

This time Duckling bravely offers.

But it turns out that Duckling
is not quite brave enough.

Poor Hedgehog.

His tricks haven't gone very well.

What's this?

Do his friends
want him to try again?

"Abracadabra!" says Hedgehog.
And a huge cake appears!

"Abracadabra!" they all say together.
And out jumps Mouse!

Hedgehog is laughing so much, he doesn't notice the cake disappearing.

All that is left on the plate is crumbs.
"I think I made the cake disappear!"
says Hedgehog.

The friends agree that Hedgehog
is very good at magic tricks.

First U.S. edition 2013

Library of Congress Catalog Card Number 2012943648

ISBN 978-0-7636-6385-8

13 14 15 16 17 18 LEO 10 9 8 7 6 5 4 3 2 1

Printed in Heshan, Guangdong, China

This book was typeset in Godlike.
The illustrations were done in pencil and digital media.

Candlewick Press
99 Dover Street
Somerville, Massachusetts 02144

visit us at www.candlewick.com